TIGER WOODS

TIGER WOODS

Golfing to Greatness

By S. A. Kramer

Random House 🏠 New York

Photograph credits: J. D. Cuban/Allsport, p. 1; Agence France Presse/Corbis-Bettmann, pp. 2, 7; V. J. Lovero/*Sports Illustrated* © Time Inc., p. 3 (top); Focus on Sports, p. 3 (bottom); Peter Read Miller/*Sports Illustrated* © Time Inc., p. 4; Albert Ferreira/Globe Photos ©, p. 5 (top); David Cannon/Allsport, p. 5 (bottom); Reuters/John Kuntz/ Archive Photos, p. 6; John Burgess/*Sports Illustrated* © Time Inc., p. 8

http://www.randomhouse.com/

Library of Congress Cataloging-in-Publication Data
Kramer, Sydelle.
Tiger Woods : golfing to greatness / by S.A. Kramer
p. cm.
Summary: Presents a biography of the professional golfer, who at the age of twenty-one became the first person of color and the youngest player to win the Masters Golf Tournament.
ISBN 0-679-88969-8 (pbk). — ISBN 0-679-98969-2 (lib. bdg.)
1. Woods, Tiger—Juvenile literature. 2. Golfers—United States— Biography—Juvenile literature. [1. Woods, Tiger. 2. Golfers.]
I. Title GV964.W66K73 1997 796.352'092—dc21 [B] 97-16974

Printed in the United States of America
10 9 8 7 6 5 4 3 2 1

to Jo

S. A. K.

CONTENTS

INTRODUCTION

What makes an athlete great? How does someone learn a sport so well that he or she knows just what to do in any game situation? Where does the determination come from that turns a jock into a champion?

Look at Tiger Woods.

He started playing golf early—so early, in fact, he learned to swing a golf club before he could even walk. By the time he was six, he was devoted to the sport. Constant hard work and practice made his child's body muscled and firm. Even before he could read, he knew how to analyze his shots and plan a winning strategy. And perhaps most importantly, he had good luck. He was born with incredible athletic talent.

To someone who doesn't know the game, golf may look like a stroll through a park. All a player has to do is swing a club at a little ball and knock it into a hole. But once you start to learn golf, you realize it requires skill, brains, and toughness like any sport. Tiger was born with the first two, but as any athlete does, he had to learn the latter.

Toughness isn't just a matter of building muscles, although staying in shape is essential. Your mind has to be tough too. Mental toughness enables you to concentrate. If athletes can't focus on what they're doing, they aren't going to win. Mental toughness also gives you confidence. If athletes don't have faith in their abilities, they can never come from behind or withstand pressure from challengers.

Tiger learned to be mentally tough before he'd even graduated from grade school. By the age of seven, he could block out all distractions and think only about what he had to do to win. He was so good at getting into a "zone"—feeling the flow of a game so intensely that he knew instinctively what to do—that sometimes after a game he couldn't even remember his shots.

Now that Tiger is an adult, golf has become his job. When that happens, some athletes stop having fun. But Tiger clearly still loves golf. No one can miss the smile on his face when he plays the game. He never seems to get bored with practice (which is a good thing, since he does it all the time), and even though he's an expert, he hasn't lost his ability to learn. That's another mark of a great athlete—never thinking you know it all.

Tiger is hungry—not just for food, although he's famous for his appetite—but for success. What drives him is his ambition to be the best. So he never gives up, no matter how far behind he is. That's the mark of a real winner—the knack of coming back.

There's something else that stamps Tiger as a great athlete. Determination. He's often the only non-Caucasian face on the links. Because of his race, he hasn't felt comfortable on every golf course. But Tiger has never let that get to him. He's played his game the best way he knows how, and has become a champion in a thoroughly white sport.

So what exactly *does* make an athlete great? There's no better answer than the remarkable life of Tiger Woods.

GOLFING IN DIAPERS

Tiger's parents knew from the start that their baby boy was special. He was born on December 30, 1975, so eager to enter the world he couldn't wait for 1976 to begin. Since there was no one else like him, his mom, Kutilda, made up a completely new name for him—Eldrick. But his dad, Earl, never called him that. He called him Tiger.

Earl had been a soldier for twenty years. When the United States sent troops to Asia to fight the Vietnam War, Earl served his country as a Green Beret lieutenant colonel. It was in Vietnam that Earl met another officer, Nguyen (NGOO-yen) T. Phong. Earl and Phong were best buddies. Phong saved Earl's life in battle. Earl nicknamed him Tiger because he was so brave and fearless. To honor his friend, Earl called his son Tiger, too.

During the Vietnam War, Earl met someone else who would change his life—Kutilda Punsawad. Tida (TEE-dah), as she was known, was from the Asian country of Thailand. Earl was divorced and had three sons, but once he met Tida, he wanted to marry again and start another family.

Earl retired from the army, and he and Tida moved to Cypress, California, a suburb of Los Angeles. At his new job he worked for a corporation that built rockets, arranging for the purchase of materials at the best price. The Woodses were the only people of color in an all-white neighborhood. Earl is a quarter Native American, a quarter Chinese, and half black. Tida is a quarter Chinese, a quarter white, and half Thai.

At first, some of their neighbors were unfriendly. People threw limes at their house. A few even fired at it with BB guns. But Earl and Tida wouldn't move. They wouldn't let anyone stop them from living where they wanted. After a while, things began to settle down.

And then Tiger was born. Somehow Earl and Tida sensed he was different from other children. After all, he was *their* baby boy. Tiger quickly became the center of their lives. They decided Tida wouldn't take a job so she could care for him full time.

Earl had a feeling his son would be athletic. Earl himself had been a terrific baseball player in his youth. He had been the only African-American to play ball for his college team. Now he was an excellent golfer. Could the old saying be true? "Like father, like son"? Earl was determined to find out.

He knew that the earlier a child masters a sport, the more accomplished he or she will be as a teenager and an adult. Tiger was only a baby, but Earl had a hunch. If he watched his dad practice now, wouldn't he naturally develop a feel for the game?

So one day, when Tiger was just six months old, Earl carried the boy and his highchair out to the garage. That was where he had set up his practice area. One side of the garage was covered with a net. Earl stood on the other side and stroked ball after ball into it.

Earl strapped Tiger into his highchair. He gave him his mashed banana and rice cereal. Then he started to practice. Tiger watched his father's every move. Earl saw Tiger watching. Maybe his hunch was correct. Earl began to dream—could Tiger become a champion golfer?

Tiger was just ten months old when Earl realized it was possible. The boy loved to crawl around dragging a sawed-off putter (a kind of golf club) behind him. Then one day Tiger stopped dragging the putter—and started swinging it instead. "His first swing was a perfect imitation of mine," Earl said.

Tiger couldn't walk yet, but he swung anything he got his hands on, from his sawed-off club to a vacuum-cleaner attachment. He had great coordination and a good eye. Once, Earl said, Tiger knocked a tennis ball "down the hall and out the back door without touching the walls." Earl believed this was a sign of great things to come.

One day father and son were in the garage.

Earl was taking a break from practice. Suddenly Tiger climbed down from his highchair and snatched a plastic putter. Eyeing the ball, he got set and smoothly swung. *Whack!* His shot sailed right into the net.

Earl ran to the house and got Tida. Tiger did it again as both parents watched. Now they knew what they had to do. Together they came up with a plan to make sure Tiger developed his talent. They also made each other a promise—Tiger would *never* be forced to play or practice. They felt that if he was ever to truly be great, he had to love golf for himself.

And he did. Tiger wouldn't let go of his first Christmas present—a golf club. By the time he was eighteen months old, he could keep score on the links. At two, he won his first tournament—wearing diapers! Tiger used sawed off clubs regular ones were taller than he was. So eager was the boy to play, he'd call Earl at work and ask, "Daddy, can I practice with you today?"

Earl and Tida weren't the only ones who thought Tiger was unusual. A television talk show heard about Tiger and invited him to appear. There he was, not quite three, smiling before the cameras, carrying the golf bag Tida had made for him. He teed off beautifully, and then out-putted the show's famous guests.

Soon Tiger was entering contests and beating ten-year-olds at the game. He quickly learned how to select the right club, and also stroked his first birdie. (In golf, every hole has a fixed number of strokes that it should take the golfer to get the ball in the cup, or pin. That fixed number is called "par." If a player needs to use more strokes, he or she is "over par." Highly skilled golfers, though, often need fewer strokes. One stroke under par is called a "birdie.")

Still, something always happened to remind Earl and Tida that Tiger was just a little boy. Once he "hit a ball into a sand trap," Tida recalled, "pulled his pants down and went pee-pee. Then he pulled his pants up and hit the shot."

But Earl and Tida's plan was working. Little Tiger was learning the game. By the age of four, he could watch the Masters (one of golf's most important tournaments) and understand what was going on. His parents realized the time had come for Tiger to get his first professional coach.

So Earl hired Rudy Duran. At first, Rudy couldn't believe what talent his pupil had. He told a reporter, "It was mind-boggling to see a four-and-a-half-year-old swinging like a pro."

Tiger's list of accomplishments grew as fast as he did. When he was five, he appeared on yet another TV show. Perfect strangers asked him for his autograph. He couldn't write script yet, so he had to print his name.

At six, Tiger shot his first hole in one (getting the ball into the cup with just one swing). He was playing simply sensational golf. Earl and Tida realized he needed new challenges. But before his game could take a leap forward, his mind had to be trained.

2

GETTING TOUGH

A golf course is like a beautiful park. There are woods and ponds and dazzling green lawns. On sunny days, a course is packed with people, most of them adults out for a good time. There are never many kids around. After all, kids don't usually care as much about golf as they do about baseball or soccer.

So imagine how startled the players on Tiger's course were when they looked up from their game and saw a small boy teeing off. A kid who didn't even come up to their waists—but who could beat the pants off almost any of them. It was truly amazing.

Earl and Tida were amazed too. Their little boy had such an extraordinary gift. But both of them knew athletic success could never be due to physical talent alone. To win, a champion had to use his mind as well as his body.

But Tiger was just a first grader. How could they teach him not to let his thoughts wander when he was playing the game? Could someone as young as he was concentrate on the golf course? Earl wanted his son to be so focused that he wouldn't pay attention to anything but his shot. The game had to be the thing, even if a herd of elephants charged by.

So Earl brought home special tapes that contained what are called "subliminal messages." Subliminal messages are words disguised so effectively by music and sound effects that the listener is often not aware he or she is hearing them. That was what happened to Tiger. When he first heard the tapes, he probably didn't notice anything special. But soon he was feeling the difference. Mixed in with soothing music and the sounds of waterfalls, waves, and wind was someone saying things like "My decisions are strong!" "I focus and give it my all!" "I believe in me!" The tapes gave Tiger messages about how to focus and feel confident.

Tiger liked them. As he listened, he stood in front of a mirror practicing his swing. He played the tapes over and over while he watched videos of old tournaments. Flutes trilled sweetly as a voice told him, "My strength is great! I will my own destiny!" He ran the tapes while practicing in the garage or putting on the carpet.

The tapes began the process of getting Tiger mentally tough. What was the best way to finish the job? Earl had an idea. While Tiger played, Earl deliberately tried to distract him. He'd jingle the coins in his pants pocket as the boy got ready to swing. If Tiger didn't react, he'd rip open the Velcro on his golf glove. Just as Tiger hit the ball, he'd drop his golf bag or caw like a crow. He'd roll balls in the way when Tiger lined up a putt.

The tricks were hard on Tiger. After all, he was just a little boy trying to play golf. He got more and more frustrated, gritting his teeth and glaring at his father. People watching thought Earl was mean. But Earl had a goal for Tiger that wasn't easy to explain. He said, "I wanted to make sure he'd never run into anybody who was tougher mentally than he was."

It took time, but the tricks began to work. No matter what Earl did, Tiger concentrated on his shot. He developed what his father called "a coldness"—a coldness that came from being tough, from putting feelings aside and getting into the rhythm of the game.

Now Tiger was playing golf for hours. He was just seven years old and could make eighty four-foot putts in a row. His confidence was growing. His focus was getting sharper. Earl and Tida had to drag him home from the course.

The first real test of how tough he was came when he was in the second grade. That's when he entered an international tournament to play against children from all over the world.

The kids were gathered on the golf course waiting for the event to begin. When Earl looked at their faces, he saw many of them were nervous. What about Tiger? Was he feeling the pressure to win?

Before Tiger teed off (hit the first stroke of a hole off a two-inch wooden peg in the ground), Earl pulled him aside. He said, "Son, I want you to know I love you no matter how you do. Enjoy yourself."

And that's what Tiger did. As he stepped up to the first tee, he was as cool as could be. His first shot was a perfect drive. Completely relaxed, he kept hitting beauties. Nothing distracted him from his pursuit of victory. Earl had worried for nothing. Tida could have told him Tiger was a secure, confident child. Their son's training was making him as mentally tough as a pro. Naturally, he won the tournament. Afterward, he told everyone, "This is how I have fun, shooting low scores."

Tiger was a natural athlete, skilled at all sports. But it was clear what was happening— his father's dreams about golf had now become his own.

3

TRAINING A TIGER

Tiger was unique. He was a third grader living two lives—one as an athlete, the other as an ordinary kid. In a way, he had learned to speak two languages—English and golf. How many other eight-year-olds could discuss pitching wedges and chips and bogeys as easily as *Star Wars*, dinosaurs, and TV?

Tiger was lucky, too. His parents were devoted to him. Earl spent hours helping him with his homework and discussing whatever the boy wanted. Tida drilled him on his multiplication tables. Not once during his childhood did they leave him with a babysitter. They refused to let anything—including money—stand in his way.

Golf is an expensive game, and Earl and Tida weren't wealthy. They had to get Tiger equipment and to pay his golf course fees and coach's salary. There were also travel expenses, as either Earl or Tida took Tiger to tournaments throughout the country.

Tiger rewarded his parents' sacrifice with victories. At eight, he won the Optimist International World Junior Championship (a title he would go on to win five more times). By the time he was eleven, he was undefeated in more than thirty California tournaments. His confidence was booming. Earl and Tida were very proud.

But Tiger didn't always have a club in his hands. He watched football, played video games, and went to the movies. There wasn't a roller coaster around he didn't want to ride. Just like his friends, he blasted rap, his favorite music. He loved watching wrestling on TV, so Earl taped matches for him that came on past his bedtime.

His parents wanted Tiger to have it both ways—to be a golf genius and also to have a normal childhood. They were careful not to spoil him. Early on, he learned about responsibility. Tida said, "If he didn't finish his homework, I wouldn't take him to the golf course." School came first—before friends, practice, and tournaments. Tida, the disciplinarian of the family, also insisted Tiger have manners. He wasn't allowed to have a temper tantrum even if he made a bad shot.

Once, during a tournament, Tiger got angry at a mistake. His temper flashing, he smacked his club against his bag. Tida quickly asked the tournament director to penalize Tiger two strokes. Tiger couldn't believe it. "Mom!" he shouted.

"Shut up," she replied. "Did the club move? Did the bag move? Who made a bad shot?" She made sure Tiger understood there was more to being a champion than winning. The best golfer in the world also had to be polite.

Earl and Tida raised Tiger to think of others, not just himself. He was a kind boy and naturally generous. When he was only nine, an awful story came on the TV news. In the African country of Ethiopia, thousands of children were starving. Tiger got very upset. Then he realized how he could help. Grabbing his piggy bank from his room, he took out twenty dollars. He donated the money to send the children food.

But there were days when it seemed Tiger thought of nothing but golf. Earl tried to get him to relax. Tiger told him, "Daddy, *this* is how I have fun." He had made up his mind to become the greatest golfer ever. He'd be better even than Jack Nicklaus, the Babe Ruth of golf.

One day, when he was eleven, Tiger rushed home from school and made a chart. It had three columns. One was a list of all the major golf tournaments. The second recorded Jack Nicklaus's age when he'd first won them. The last was blank. Tiger would put *his* age there when *he* won the tournaments. His goal was to be younger than Nicklaus when he won each. Up went the chart right over his bed.

But Earl and Tida knew Tiger was up against more than Nicklaus had ever been. Tiger was black and Asian. It was the 1980s, but a person of color had never been a golfing superstar. Nicklaus was white in a game that had always been a white man's sport.

Golf first started over five hundred years ago in Scotland. It didn't cross the sea to America until 1888. For years, it wasn't especially popular here. It was so expensive to play, most people couldn't afford it. Even today, a good set of golf clubs will cost thousands of dollars. A putter alone can cost more than $200. Almost all the courses belonged to private country clubs controlled by well-to-do white men. Many of these clubs charged a high fee to join. They did not accept people of color, or women, as members.

Just like baseball, golf had to be integrated. It wasn't until 1975 that a black golfer played in the Masters! By the 1980s, most clubs had opened their doors to minorities, but some around the country still discriminated.

Earl knew that if Tiger was to be a champ, the boy would have to break down racial barriers His own experience had taught him how difficult that could be. When he had traveled with his college ball club in the 1950s, he hadn't been allowed to sleep or eat with his teammates. Many hotels and restaurants were segregated. In some places it was against the law for restaurants to serve both blacks and whites and for hotels to rent rooms to both races.

Earl never forgot the prejudice he had experienced. More than anything, he must have wanted to protect his son from this pain. But he couldn't. When Tiger practiced at clubs near their home, there were times people stared at him. They weren't used to seeing people of color on the links. Even in school, race was a problem. Tiger was the only black child in his kindergarten. As he got older, white kids sometimes picked on him. Once a bunch of them tied him to a tree.

But Tiger himself was convinced his color didn't matter. He was sure if he won, all of golf's doors would open to him. He loved the game and couldn't imagine not playing it. Black, white, or purple, Asian, African, or Caucasian, he was going to take the golfing world by storm.

By the age of twelve, Tiger had mastered all the shots. He could hit long drives as high as home runs, or screaming liners a few feet off the ground. His balls would go from right to left or left to right, with backspin or without. His approach shots (hitting the ball from the fairway to the green) were steady, and his short putts found the cup.

He was as at home on the golf course as he was in his own house. Nothing made him feel quite as good as hitting the ball just right. He would stroll down the lush lawns, breathing in the fresh air, planning his next shot, analyzing the game. Which direction was the wind blowing? Where would it take his ball? How much did the land slope? Would the ball roll left or right when it came down?

Golf is a complicated game, but the teenage Tiger seemed fearless. In August 1989, he entered his first national tournament, the 21st Insurance Golf Classic in Arkansas. Only thirteen years old, he was up against much older golfers. Some were professionals, some adult amateurs. Would the pressure finally get to him? Tiger went out there and enjoyed himself. He ended up finishing second, beating eight pros.

The Woods family living room was getting crowded with trophies. Tiger made winning look easy—but even he could get an attack of nerves, especially the night before a tournament. Despite all his training, Tiger sometimes had problems concentrating on the course. Sometimes he started his game slowly, as if he had to warm up, like a car. Although he never rushed his shots, he slashed wild ones now and then. They'd zoom off the fairway (the wide, open lawn that starts off each hole) and into the woods. If he wasn't focused, he lost control, and then his drives weren't long and straight. They'd land in the rough (tall grass, rocks, and bushes), a bunker (an obstacle, often a long dent in the grass filled with sand), or a water hazard (a pond or a stream). He minded his manners, as his mother had taught him, but an observer could see frustration in his face and body language.

Tough as he was, it was clear that Tiger could be tougher. If golf was to be his life, his concentration had to get even more intense. The greatest athletes understand they have to shrug off their mistakes. Tiger had to learn to do just that.

That year, Tiger met a sports psychologist named Jay Brunza. A sports psychologist helps athletes sharpen the mental part of their game. A player who gets distracted doesn't win. His confidence sinks. He no longer trusts his instincts. The doctor spent time talking with

Tiger. He came out to the links with him and watched him play. He even hypnotized Tiger! Tiger enjoyed it. And his game got stronger.

The next year was a big one—he'd be going to high school. Tiger was growing up. It was time to make his move.

4

THE BUZZ BEGINS

Summer 1990. Tiger's classmates were on vacation. But Tiger was working—playing golf. Ever since he could remember, he'd done the same thing each year. Along with other junior golfers, he hit the road. All across the country, there were important tournaments to play. He entered as many as he could.

Tiger was fourteen now—no longer Earl and Tida's little boy. He knew more about golf than many pros. He was so mature, he made his own travel arrangements, even setting up his practice times and choosing caddies (a caddy carries a golfer's bag and often helps him select a club or decide how to approach his next shot). Earl was delighted. He said, "Tiger's been trained to make his own decisions and take responsibility for them."

His game was going well. With his slender, well-built body, Tiger moved gracefully over the course. When he swung, he had perfect form. Fans were entranced by his good looks and smooth appearance. His clothes never seemed wrinkled. Even his shoes looked clean!

As Tiger walked from hole to hole, he had a wide smile for everyone. When he took a bad shot, it never got him down for long. He'd just snap off a long, perfect drive, and his whole mood would seem to change. He'd even cheer for his own shots. It seemed once he got going, he was impossible to stop.

But behind his warm brown eyes and friendly face, Tiger was steely in his will to win. Tida, his greatest fan, encouraged his competitive streak. "When you are ahead," she told him, "don't take it easy, kill them. After the finish, then be a sportsman."

The competition on the tour was fierce. Tiger's emotions ran high while his body wore down. He said, "I like the feeling of trying my hardest under pressure. But it's so intense... it feels like a lion is tearing at my heart."

The summer tour was hectic and expensive. By September, Earl and Tida had spent thousands of dollars, and Tiger was exhausted. But he had won event after event. He was so good that one of his golf teachers said, "Tiger comes from another world."

Word was getting out. Sports agents were calling, asking to sign Tiger up. Even the pros, so much older and more experienced than the teenaged Tiger, were taking notice. One called him "awesome."

Tiger didn't let the fuss get to him. He told reporters, "I'm glad to get back in school and be with my friends."

It was his first year at Anaheim Western High School, and Tiger wanted to do well. He had always taken his studies seriously. As the term went on, he earned close to straight A's. Of course, he didn't stop playing golf. He was on the school team.

Then when he was fifteen, the buzz suddenly got louder. *Sports Illustrated* ran a story on him. He was a young black face in an older white crowd, an Asian athlete in a country where Asian athletes are rare. But Tiger made it clear to reporters he didn't want to be labeled racially or ethnically. He said, "I don't want to be the best black golfer on the tour. I want to be the best *golfer* on the tour."

Some experts thought Tiger was getting a little ahead of himself. After all, he hadn't yet won a single national title. And there were times he still played like a kid. He made silly mistakes. Instead of taking safe shots, he took unnecessary chances.

Still, Earl was confident Tiger would prove the buzz true. He believed his son's career was "all being controlled by the Man upstairs." But he also understood Tiger's talent better than anyone—more than Tiger's coaches, more even than Tida. After all, Earl had studied Tiger's game for years. He often traveled to tournaments with the boy—Tiger was too young to go alone. Father and son were so close that Tiger felt Earl was his best buddy. Now Earl had a sense Tiger was about to take off.

But on July 28, 1991, it looked as if Earl and the buzz were dead wrong. Tiger was competing in the U.S. Junior Amateur Championship in Orlando, Florida. After six holes in the last round, Tiger was three strokes down. He was running out of time. If he was going to catch the leader, he had to make his move now. Many golfers his age would have folded there and then.

Tiger, though, had a mysterious inner strength. It had to do with his supreme self-confidence. With his never-give-up style, he came back to take the lead. But when his concentration faded on the eighteenth (and last) hole, he had to settle for a tie.

Now he would have to compete in a playoff. In golf, a playoff has no time limit. In a way, it's like baseball. As long as the score remains tied, the athletes keep playing. A tournament isn't over until one golfer reaches the cup in fewer strokes than the other.

Tiger wanted to win on the first playoff hole. His instincts told him which clubs to use, and how to make the shot. As he does when he's playing his best, he was in a zone—thinking with his body, and not his mind.

It worked! Tiger won the event on the first

hole. When it was over, he was so tired that he couldn't talk. Later, he said, "I never dreamed the pressure would be that great." He was the youngest golfer—and the first person of color—ever to win the Junior Am.

Tiger was feeling good—so good, in fact, he was a little full of himself. "I want to become the Michael Jordan of golf," he told a reporter. "I want to be the best ever."

The buzz was getting louder.

5

SLOWDOWN

Everyone in golf was talking about Tiger. The winner of six junior titles, he was the youngest golfer ever to be named the American Junior Golf Association's Player of the Year. Experts were comparing him to Jack Nicklaus. Tiger was on a high.

Things got even better when he arrived in Los Angeles in February 1992. Tiger had been invited to the Nissan Open at the Riviera Country Club. When he teed off on February 27, he became the youngest golfer in history to appear in a PGA (Professional Golfers' Association) tournament. Just a high school sophomore, he was playing on a new level now—with pros. But unlike his opponents, he had to get permission to miss school to play.

Some people were angry that Tiger was there. Phone calls were made threatening his life. As Tiger played a round, three security guards followed him. He joked, "Sixteen years old, and I've already had my first death threat."

The fans at the Nissan Open were crazy about him. They loved to watch his sweet, smooth swing. Even though he was thin, he had tremendous power. He flicked the club around like a whip because he moved his shoulders more than his hips. From start to finish, his swing made a perfect circle.

A gallery of three thousand trailed him around the course (in golf, the crowd is called a "gallery"). Only a thin rope separated them from Tiger. People fixed their eyes on his determined face, partially hidden by a hat. No one guessed he was wearing contact lenses.

But they couldn't miss Tiger's bag. His driver (the club used for teeing off) stuck out among the fourteen clubs. It had a cover that looked like a tiger. Tida had made it for him. On it, she had stitched LOVE FROM MOM in Thai.

Wherever Tiger went, course officials followed. They held up white paddles with QUIET PLEASE written on them. But the crowd didn't always pay attention. At times they chanted "You the kid!" at Tiger. One man kept flashing a sign: GO GET'UM TIGER. Even if he hit a bad shot, everyone applauded.

Some fans ran from shot to shot so they could be in the front to watch. There were TV cameras moving around and newspaper photographers popping flashbulbs. With all the hubbub, it was a good thing Tiger had learned to ignore distractions.

In the gallery was a group of Tiger's friends— his high school golf team had come to cheer him on. None of them wanted to miss this big event, so they were all there.

The crowd stared at Tiger and thought he looked calm. What they couldn't know was how nervous he was inside. After all, he was competing against some of the best golfers in the world. He said, "I was so tense, I had a tough time holding the club." Tida understood, reminding reporters, "He's just a kid."

The Nissan Open wasn't Tiger's event. Up

against the pros, he could see the flaws in his game. His major weakness was his inability to control the distance of his shots. He swung too hard at times and couldn't place the ball properly. Although he insisted he was "icy under pressure," it seemed his emotions were still getting in his way, and that he wasn't always thinking clearly about his next shot.

It soon became obvious Tiger wasn't going to make the cut. (Only a certain number of golfers in a tournament are allowed to move into the final rounds.) Still, he didn't lose his sense of humor. When he got himself into a rough spot on one hole, he pulled a club out of his bag and strolled over to the fans. Holding out the club, he cracked, "Anyone want to try it?"

Before he went home, Tiger met with reporters. Many expected him to feel bad, but he was smiling. "It was a learning experience," he said, "and I learned I'm not that good....I've got a lot of growing to do."

Tiger had come back down to earth.

Naturally, he was anxious when he started his summer tour. His Junior Am championship was on the line. He was defending the title at the

Wollaston Golf Club in Massachusetts. No golfer in history had ever won the Junior Am twice.

The biggest crowd in Junior Am history—over a thousand fans—was waiting for Tiger at the course. Some people had driven 150 miles to see him play. As usual, he started slowly, then picked up the pace. Still, he was two shots behind in the final round with only six holes to play.

Suddenly his competition faded. It was as though Tiger was meant to win. On the 18th hole, the victory was complete. Earl came out on the green (the grassy area around the cup) and embraced his son. The fans clapped wildly. Now that the tournament was over, Tiger admitted, "You just cannot believe how much tension I was feeling."

Tiger was triumphant—but the tour went on. This summer it seemed endless. When he got home after a tournament, he'd be exhausted. Friends would call, but he was too tired to go out. In his spare time, he'd just rest in his room. It turned out Tiger wasn't just tired. He was so stressed out, he couldn't gain weight. While he'd gotten taller and taller—in the last two years, he'd spurted up six and a half inches—he weighed only 140 pounds. At six foot one, he was too skinny to be truly strong. He had to get heavier to build up his stamina.

In an effort to put on the pounds, he stuffed himself at McDonald's. He also loved pizza. But even wolfing down pizza, strawberry milk shakes, and vanilla ice cream cones didn't beef him up. The strain of being young and a champion golfer was starting to show.

Then in the last tournament of the year, Tiger actually gave up on a game. It was his seventeenth birthday, but he wasn't celebrating. Instead, he was playing in the final round at the 1992 Orange Bowl International Junior Invitational in Coral Gables, Florida. Something was wrong. He was swinging as though he didn't want to be there. No matter what club he used, he just couldn't hit the ball right. After a while, it seemed clear he'd stopped trying.

Earl was furious. As soon as he was alone with Tiger, he let his son have it. "Who do you think you are?" he screamed. "You *never* quit! Do you understand me?"

Tiger must have felt awful. He was must also

have been frightened of Earl's anger. Hours went by before he spoke a word. But he learned a valuable lesson. He never gave up again.

Tiger was lucky. The incident didn't hurt his reputation. The magazine *Golf World* named him Player of the Year. But a number of pros began wondering if so much buzz was bad for Tiger. Should someone as young and inexperienced as he was get so much attention?

After all, they said, reporters were following him everywhere, even though he was still just a teenager. Fans always expected to see him at the top of his game. Newspapers and magazines were calling him great—but he hadn't proved himself against the best. Maybe Tiger was trying to do too much too soon.

It was 1993. No one was listening to the pros. But soon it would be clear that they were right.

6

COMEBACK

Tiger wanted it all—to be the best in the game, a top student, and one of the gang. And for a while, he seemed to be doing just that.

He never missed a practice and still got A's and B's in school. One of his teachers said, "He was a very competitive young man who wanted to be the best, no matter what it was. If he didn't get the top grade in class, he studied harder the next week." He also had an active social life. In the spring of 1993, seventeen-year-old Tiger had a girlfriend and a car.

Then his life came to a halt, just as the pros had feared. In June, he got mononucleosis, a virus that causes a high fever, swollen glands, and a terrible sore throat. He was more tired than he had ever been before. The illness left him so weak that it was three weeks before he had the energy to practice again.

But he recovered in time to play in the 1993 Junior Am. If he won again this year, he'd be the first golfer ever to take the title three times.

Ready for anything, he arrived at the Waverly Country Club in Portland, Oregon. There was a record crowd of 4,650 for the final round. They came to see a showdown between Tiger and another young golfer named Ryan Armour.

Tiger must have known that up to now, this was the most important round of golf he had played. He had asked Jay Brunza to be his caddy, so he had his personal sports psychologist out on the links with him today.

It was a good move on Tiger's part, since he got off to his usual slow start. By the 17th hole, he was down two strokes. Now he was going to have to stage a comeback to win the championship.

Tiger played the 17th well, and had a chance for a birdie. With his ball eight feet from the cup, it was do or die. Before he putted, he consulted with Jay. Then he said, "Got to be like Nicklaus. Got to will this in the hole."

The inch-and-a half ball must have seemed so tiny to Tiger at that moment. What if he swung at it and missed? It weighed just an ounce and a half—so easy to hit too hard. The cup itself was just four inches deep and four and a quarter inches wide—it is harder to sink a putt than to make a basket!

The gallery was hushed. Would Tiger come through? Nobody was better at putting in the clutch. He put his head down, straightened his legs, and spread his feet apart. Then he struck the ball with his putter. Perfect hit! It slid over the grass and plopped into the cup. Birdie!

Now he was just one stroke behind. This tournament wasn't over yet. If Tiger could birdie the 18th hole too, he'd have a chance to tie Ryan.

Tiger's focus was sharp. He slammed a long drive off the tee. Standing nearby, Earl was delighted. "He airmailed it," he said.

The ball sailed over 300 yards. No wonder Tiger was famous for the length of his shots. One of his caddies had once said, after Tiger hit a drive, "That ball doesn't want to come down."

The drive was long—but it wasn't perfect. The ball landed in a rough by the side of the fairway. Tiger grabbed a three-iron (an easy-to-handle club that drives the ball far and high) from his bag and hit an approach shot. It plunked down in a bunker. Had his luck finally run out?

The ball was forty yards from the green. Now Tiger had his work cut out for him. To have a chance at a birdie, he had to put his next stroke near the cup. That meant a long bunker shot— one of golf's hardest. Many in the crowd thought Tiger was through.

It was the kind of pressure only a great athlete can handle. Tiger swung his club and pounded the ball out of the sand. When the ball landed, it was just ten feet from the hole.

One more shot and the birdie was his. Tiger said, "It's either make the putt or go home." Using the same routine he'd followed since he was six, he took two practice strokes, looked at the target, looked at the ball, then back at the target, then back at the ball. Finally, he putted.

The ball dipped into the hole! The crowd went wild. Who would have believed it? Tie!

Now Tiger and Ryan squared off in the playoff. On the very first hole, a self-assured Tiger turned the heat up. He slapped a drive that landed only twenty feet from the cup. His next shot put him just four feet away. On his third stroke, he sank the putt.

Ryan couldn't make the hole in three shots— he needed four. Tiger's comeback was complete! Earl raced onto the green, and father and son hugged and cried. "I did it. I did it," Tiger blurted. All choked up, Earl replied, "I'm so proud of you." Later, Tiger told reporters, "It was the most amazing comeback of my entire career. I had to play the best two holes of my life...and I did it."

7

THE SWING DOCTOR

But the sweet taste of victory didn't last long. At the end of the summer, Tiger lost the 1993 U.S. Amateur Championship. He must have been more than disappointed—if Tiger was going to be a great golfer, the Amateur was one title he had to win.

His swing had started to give him trouble. Something had to be done, and fast. So Earl hired a man named Butch Harmon. Butch was a "swing doctor." He'd teach Tiger better technique.

Butch didn't fool around. He insisted Tiger learn how to make the length of his shots consistent. Because of Butch, Tiger widened his stance when he swung. He began to turn his hips less, so his swing tightened up. Instead of constantly using all his power, he slowed his stroke down. Suddenly, Tiger had more control over the ball.

Experts thought Tiger's swing was close to perfect. When he got ready to tee off, he kept his head down, his eye on the ball. Spreading his legs, he planted his feet firmly. His hands gripped the driver tightly about an inch from the top.

Swinging right-handed, Tiger kept his arms completely straight. He swept the club back as far and high as he was able. With his left arm flung up, his left shoulder nearly brushed his lips. Then he swung the driver down as his hips swiveled, slamming the ball hard with his quick, strong hands.

The swing twisted his body in the direction the ball flew. All his power and speed pulled his weight from his right foot to his left. As he followed through, his right knee bent forward but his left leg stayed straight. The club came through so high, his right shoulder grazed his chin. But his motion didn't stop until the driver was behind his head. It looped so far back that it touched the back of his neck.

The swing was graceful and packed a real punch. The ball rocketed long and straight down the fairway. After he'd seen it, one pro said, "It's hard to believe anybody hits the ball that far."

But the swing left Tiger's feet in a peculiar position, almost as though he'd been in an accident. His right foot turned with his body and then slid up on its toes, like a ballet dancer's. Yet his left foot was still flat, and seemed glued to the ground. It didn't point to where the ball had gone but to the tee.

Butch knew champions weren't made from beautiful swings alone. So he taught Tiger to pay better attention to the weather. Was it a clear, sunny day? That's when the ball would shoot off the tee like a bullet. Or was the air damp and humid, making everything, the ball included, heavier?

What about the grass? If it was wet and the ground soggy, the ball wouldn't skip or roll much. But if it was dry and the lawns hard, the ball would bounce as if it was on a trampoline. How about the temperature? Hot weather slowed a ball down, cool air sped it up. And what if there was a breeze? A strong wind could blow the ball around like a kite.

Butch helped Tiger make his game stronger. First Earl, then Jay, now Butch—Team Tiger, as it became known, was in place. With these guys on his side, Tiger must have felt ready for anything.

8

YEAR OF THE TIGER

Spring 1994. Tiger was graduating from high school. With his close-to-A average, he'd won the Dial Award as America's top scholar-athlete. Now it was on to college, where he'd major in economics. The winner of a full scholarship, he was going to Stanford University in Palo Alto, California.

But that was in the fall. First, he had some golfing to do. It was that time again—the summer tour. Tiger played in a selection of tournaments to warm up for the big one—the 1994 U.S. Amateur. If he took the championship, he'd be the first player ever to win both the Junior Am and the Amateur. Only eighteen years old, he'd also be the youngest player to take home the trophy. And no black or Asian-American golfer had ever won it before.

The Amateur began on Thursday, August 25, 1994. There were big crowds at the Tournament Players Club–Sawgrass Stadium in Ponte Vedra Beach, Florida. No one could miss the determined look on Tiger's face. He easily qualified for the final round on Sunday. He would face an excellent golfer, Trip Kuehne.

Sunday was hot and humid. Dragonflies and mosquitoes buzzed all around the course. Tiger was dressed for the heat in shorts and a red-and-white striped polo shirt. His white shoes and socks gleamed in the sun. Instead of his usual cap, he wore a straw hat with a wide black band.

The Amateur final was two rounds—thirty-six holes. Jay Brunza was Tiger's caddy, whispering encouragement and advice. Clutching his walking stick, Earl trailed them to every hole. He wasn't going to miss a thing.

But after just thirteen holes, Tiger was down by six. His concentration seemed wobbly. He was hitting balls off the fairway into the woods. It was still just the first round, but it seemed impossible that he could still win. No one had ever come from so far behind to win the Amateur.

But no one was quite like Tiger.

At the lunch break, he showered and changed his clothes. It gave him the feeling of making a new start. As the second round began, Earl was heard to whisper in Tiger's ear, "Let the legend grow."

Tiger bore down and seemed to rediscover his confidence. After six holes, he had cut Trip's lead to five. Now he was really focused. There wasn't much time left. It was as though he couldn't get going until he was in big trouble.

With nine holes to go, Tiger was still three down. It never occurred to him to give up— he just kept coming back. Somewhere inside him, he must have known he could pull it out. And sure enough, he birdied the 16th hole to tie Trip.

The 17th hole was dangerous. Tiger would win or lose the title here. Known as the Island Hole, the 17th hole had a short fairway and a green surrounded by water. From the tee to the hole, it was only 139 yards. But a bad shot, or a misreading of the wind, would put the ball into the water, and Tiger would be penalized one stroke.

Tiger seemed uncertain about which club to use. The breeze was strong. What kind of shot should he take? Taking some practice swings with his nine-iron (a club used for a short approach shot), he felt the wind suddenly slow and shift. Now it was softly blowing from behind him.

That seemed to do it. Tiger snatched a club called a pitching wedge and stepped to the tee. A golfer doesn't normally use a wedge unless he's stuck in a bunker. But Tiger knew a wedge shot would sail high and, with its backspin, hardly roll at all. So he had a chance to clear the pond on a fly without the ball rolling back into the water when it landed.

The shot was a big gamble. "I was going directly at the pin," he said. If it worked, he'd be on the green in one stroke and could birdie the hole. If it didn't, he'd probably lose the title.

The crowd around the teeing ground knew what Tiger was going to try. Everyone got quiet, as if they were holding their breath. At home in

California, Tida was watching her son on TV. She was so nervous, her heart was pounding.

Tiger smacked the ball off the tee. It flew high in the air like a bird over the water. When it came down, it took one hop on the green, spun back a little, and came to rest three feet from the edge.

The shot worked! Tida couldn't believe it. She rolled off the bed and onto the floor. "That boy almost gave me a heart attack," she said later. "All I kept saying was 'God, don't let that ball go in the water.'"

But Tiger hadn't won the hole yet. There was a birdie to make. To do that, he had to sink a fourteen-foot putt.

Jay removed the flag that marked the cup. Tiger studied the grass and the tilt of the green. Then as though it were no problem, he calmly hit the ball. As he watched it whirl toward the cup, his mouth fell open.

Birdie! Tiger kicked up his left foot and slugged the air with his right arm. Now he had the lead.

There was one more hole to go, but it seemed easy by comparison. The greatest comeback in the history of the Amateur was complete. The crowd cheered for the champion. Tiger would go home with the trophy.

Trip was a gracious loser. He gave Tiger a high-five and a hug. Earl dropped his walking stick and cried, then embraced his son on the green. He told Tiger, "You have done something no black person has ever done, and you will forever be a part of history."

Later, Tiger talked about the tournament with reporters. He didn't remember the shot that cleared the water, or pumping his fist after the putt. That's because, he said, "I was in the zone." As always, he went out of his way to compliment his opponent. He commented, "It's an amazing feeling to come from that many down to beat a great player."

It seemed as if everyone wanted to congratulate Tiger. Jesse Jackson called him. Sinbad phoned. Tiger's hometown of Cypress gave him the key to the city. Television talk shows invited him to appear.

But Tiger didn't go before the cameras. He had more important things to do. He was getting ready to go to college.

9

FIRST TIME AT THE MASTERS

Tiger was a champion golfer, but at Stanford he wasn't the only great athlete around. The university has a long tradition of educating winners, from Olympic medalists to Hall of Famers. It sets high academic standards, and its students are among the best and brightest. As Tiger said, "There are *geniuses* here."

While people mobbed him on the golf course, his college classmates left him alone. On campus, he was just another first-year student. Between studying for his classes and playing for the Stanford golf team, Tiger didn't have much spare time. But he made sure to have fun now and then—he went to every party he could. Sometimes he relaxed by biking sixty miles along the California coast.

At first, the golf team must have made Tiger uncomfortable. After all, he was a freshman, and everyone else was a senior. As the rookie, he had to carry his teammates' bags and sleep in the worst hotel bed when the team traveled. But what he liked least was being the butt of his teammates' jokes. When he wore his glasses instead of contacts, they teased him by calling him Urkel (after the nerdy kid on *Family Matters*). Tiger really hated that.

Some of his teammates felt Tiger had trouble fitting in. Though he was never rude, he could be cold. He often kept to himself and didn't have much to say. Seemingly slow to trust people, Tiger didn't open up until he got to know them. But he was always happy to help anyone who needed golfing advice.

Tiger's growing fame was a burden. Reporters were always calling for interviews. Strangers picked on him because he was famous. They sent him hate mail—letters full of insults, curse words, and threats. Then in December, he was mugged on campus by a man who knew who he was. The thief grabbed him from behind and said, "Tiger, give me your wallet." Then he slugged Tiger in the mouth with a knife handle. He stole Tiger's watch and a gold chain Tida had given him.

Tiger was okay. And despite the robbery, 1994 didn't end badly. He was named *Golf World*'s Man of the Year. He also won the *Los Angeles Times* Player of the Year Award. Not bad for a college freshman and an amateur golfer.

But Tiger knew 1995 would be a challenge. For the first time, he'd be competing in three major PGA events. Winning the Amateur had qualified him to play in the Masters, the U.S. Open, and the British Open. The top golfers in the world would be on the links. On average, they were twenty years older than Tiger, who was only nineteen.

The Masters came first. America's greatest tournament, it is held every year at the Augusta National Golf Club in Augusta, Georgia. The course is tricky and difficult, famous for its quick greens. A putt that is accurate anywhere else skids right by the cup here.

**Despite the fact that his stance looks awkward,
experts agree that Tiger's swing is nearly perfect.**

Even when surrounded by fans, noise, and other distractions,
Tiger must keep his concentration and stay focused.

Tiger has told reporters that his father, Earl, is his best friend.

One of Tiger's biggest fans is his mother, Tida, who shows her support in this picture by wearing red.

From the time Tiger was two years old
and won his first tournament, his parents knew
that he was a winner.

Tiger enjoys the opening of the Official All Star Cafe
with Monica Seles and Luke Perry.

One of Tiger's dreams
for the future
is to bring golf to
inner-city youth.

Tiger Woods becomes the youngest golfer ever to win the Masters—and with the record lowest score, too!

Tiger is all smiles as 1996 Masters champion Nick Faldo helps him into his green jacket.

Tiger in heaven!

Tiger was busy with classes. But he knew he'd do badly at the Masters unless he prepared. So on top of his schoolwork, he began to train hard. To do well, he had to learn to control the speed of his putts. That was why he practiced at the Stanford gym instead of a golf course. The gym's polished wooden floors were as slippery and hard as the Masters greens.

Tiger spent months getting ready for Augusta. Just before the tournament began, he had to cram for final exams too. Earl and Tida realized he was feeling the pressure. Before he left, Tiger watched a tape of an old Masters. Sitting in front of the TV, he suddenly felt sick. His stomach was killing him, as though he'd eaten something rotten. But it wasn't bad food. It was nerves.

Yet when the Masters started on April 6, 1995, there was Tiger, healthy and smiling. As he entered the clubhouse, he must have felt the past all around him. After all, these were the links of legend. The sport's greatest golfers had all been winners here, putting on the green jacket that's awarded instead of a trophy. They had played with pride on one of the world's most beautiful courses, where the earth rolled in waves just like the ocean.

Tiger smelled the sweet air, perfumed by magnolias and pines. He saw the huge oaks lining the lawns, along with bright azaleas and dogwood. There were wide fairways, steep slopes, and fast-running creeks. The grass on the greens was shorter than a buzz cut.

The Masters was a tournament of champions. Yet for decades, it had been an American disgrace. It wasn't long ago that blacks weren't welcome here.

Tiger was the first black amateur to ever play in the tournament. In sixty-one years, only three other black golfers had walked this course. No black man had played here since 1988. The Augusta National itself had admitted no black members until 1990. With every stroke, Tiger would be making history here.

As if to show how proud he was of his heritage as a black, an Asian, and an American, Tiger appeared on the links with a special black leather golf bag. On it was the name UNITED STATES printed in gold. When it rained during the first round, he opened a red, white, and blue umbrella, complete with little white stars shining out of the blue.

After the second round, he left the Augusta National and practiced on a public course where black caddies played. Earl explained why his son wanted to go there. He said, "We are acknowledging that we know who came before Tiger and that they suffered humiliation and that we realize the debt. It's a way of saying thank you and a promise to carry the baton."

But despite past Masters prejudice, Tiger was thrilled to be there. Earl followed him around, videotaping all his shots. He had trouble controlling his short irons (the clubs used for clearing a hazard or to make a short approach shot to the green), but his drives were astonishingly long. The defending Masters champ said, "I had to use binoculars to see how far the ball was going."

Now six foot two, Tiger was swinging faster and harder than anyone else. His long legs and quick shoulders helped him pound the ball over three hundred yards. It blasted into the air so fast, no one could see it coming off the club. Like Michael Jordan floating toward the basket, the ball looked as if it would never come down.

But people could hear it. When Tiger hammered it, the ball swooshed through the air with a whine. No other golfer's ball sounded quite like it.

Tiger had fun at the Masters, but he didn't yet have the experience to win. He wasn't disappointed. No one knew better that he was still learning the game. Besides, he'd done something to be proud of—he'd made his first PGA cut. He'd be back soon. And one day he'd win.

As soon as the tournament ended, Tiger left for Stanford. He had a history exam at 9 A.M. the next morning. But back in California, he apparently couldn't stop thinking about the Masters. He decided to send Augusta National officials a thank-you note. His time there, he wrote, was "the most wonderful week of my life." Even more, he said, "It is here that I left my youth behind and became a man."

The Masters had once been closed to people like Tiger. It was ready to change—and he was the man to do it.

10

SETBACK

Something was happening—Tiger was exhausted.
Right after the Masters, he simply tried to do too
much. He was playing golf all the time, appear-
ing in college tournaments and entering PGA
events. But he wasn't just a full-time athlete—he
was also going to school.

Tiger seemed to be burning out. His grades
had slipped to a B average.

His golf game was suffering too. When he
made bad shots now, he often lost his temper. In
more than one college tournament, he smacked
his bag and threw his clubs. Once he was so
angry, he broke a club.

The experts started asking questions about Tiger once more. Was he injuring himself by swinging too hard? After all, he'd recently hurt his back and had had a knee operation. His shoulder bothered him on occasion. Did he have enough stamina to become a pro? He'd put on some weight, but was still only 150 pounds. Then there was the cost of fame—being constantly in the spotlight was grueling. Was Tiger all too human—was his body already wearing out?

On June 16, 1995, it seemed as if they might be right. Tiger was playing in the U.S. Open at Shinnecock Hills in New York. He'd smacked a shot into a deep rough on the 6th hole of the second round. Playing an iron, he swung hard— too hard—to blast the ball back onto the grass. He suddenly felt a sharp pain in his left wrist.

The tournament was over for Tiger. He had sprained his wrist. Now it was clear his schedule was too hectic. Some people wondered if it was Earl's fault. Could he be pushing Tiger too hard? He was the one who had shaped his son's career—was Tiger being crushed under Earl's thumb?

Sometimes it seemed to people that Earl had no life of his own. Retired from his job, he followed Tiger around so closely, he jokingly called himself "The Shadow." In his wallet was a snapshot of the boy at ten months, swinging a vacuum cleaner attachment. Whenever the time seemed right, he pulled it out to show reporters. Was Earl living through Tiger?

Earl made no secret of his ambitions for his son. Friends said he was a loving father trying to help Tiger the best that he could. Everyone agreed it wasn't easy raising a boy wonder.

Tiger himself never considered blaming Earl for his problems. He couldn't imagine life without his dad. "We're best friends," he said.

As usual, Tiger drew a lesson from his loss and injury at the Open. He told reporters, "I learned I have to manage my game a little better. I can't keep going for broke."

Tiger was down—but hardly out.

BACK ON TOP

When the British Open at St. Andrews in Scotland began July 20, Tiger seemed to be in excellent spirits, fully recovered from the sprain. He didn't come close to taking the title, but the competition was good practice for him. He must have had September's U.S. Amateur on his mind—he'd be going for two wins in a row.

The twisting winds in Scotland taught Tiger a lesson in ball control. He learned there was more to winning than driving a shot over 300 yards. When he arrived in Newport, Rhode Island, for the 1995 Amateur, he didn't worry at all about the tricky gusts off its bay.

Tiger practically took over the Newport

Country Club. A thousand fans trailed him around the course. They walked down the fairways beside him, so close they could see his long eyelashes and dazzling white teeth.

Sunday was the final round. Jay Brunza was Tiger's caddy. The day was gray, and the waves on the bay were swirling. But at least it wasn't raining, and the course was hard and fast.

Tiger walked out of the yellow clubhouse and got ready to tee off. As always, his shirt was neatly tucked into belted pants, his short hair curled underneath a cap.

To make his stroke loose and relaxed, he did some stretching exercises. The stretching also prevented him from pulling a muscle. Then he put a white glove on his left hand. His right was completely bare, except for a strip of white tape neatly wound around his middle finger.

Tiger looked over the 1st hole. The wind was blowing. To gauge its direction, he pulled out a clump of grass and threw it in the air. Gripping his driver, he hooked his right pinky under the second finger of his left hand. He looked so comfortable out there, it was as if he had been born to play golf.

But after twelve holes of the two-round final, Tiger had fallen three strokes behind. He refused to panic. He started playing by instinct, using his full array of shots.

Sure enough, Tiger surged ahead by the 24th hole. But the tournament was close—by the 36th (and last) hole, his lead was only one. The neck-and-neck finish only brought out Tiger's best.

Teeing off with a two-iron (a hard-to-handle club used to make a long drive), he slugged the ball 265 yards. Now he had to make a great approach shot, or risk being tied. The green was 140 yards away, sitting on a rise.

Tiger went to his bag and pulled out an eight-iron (one of the clubs called "short irons"). He swung it so fast and hard, fans heard the club whir through the air. There was a crack, and a divot (a clump of grass and dirt) kicked high. The ball ripped out over the lawn.

When it finally stopped, it was within eighteen inches of the cup. An easy putt—but Tiger took nothing for granted. He clutched the putter barehanded, his glove stuffed in the back left pocket of his pants. Gently, he flicked the club at the ball.

In! He was only nineteen years old, but he'd just won back-to-back Amateur championships. Earl ran out on the green and jumped into his son's arms. After the trophy was presented, he toasted the boy with champagne. He said proudly, "To my son, Tiger. One of the greatest golfers in the history of the United States."

How could anyone doubt Tiger again?

12

TO BE OR NOT TO BE A PRO

Spring 1996. Tiger was finishing his second year at Stanford. But people were beginning to wonder: Would he be back for a third? Most reporters believed Tiger was considering turning pro.

He had, after all, just spent months building up his strength, working out regularly with 250-pound weights. And he'd put on some weight—he was up to 155 pounds. His shoulders were wider than ever, and his arms were thick with muscles.

Tiger had worked on his game too. Butch found him an eager pupil. Tiger had added a new and deadly stroke to his stockpile of weapons—a long, low shot that barely curved and landed without spin. Now he had even more control over the ball. His drives had also improved—still powerful off the tee, but more accurate and consistent. Golf, Tiger was realizing, wasn't only about strength—to win, a player had to also develop a soft touch.

In April, he played in his second Masters, but didn't do well enough to make the cut. He wasn't patient with his putts, and he paid the price. During the tournament, his mind seemed to be on other things. Reporters badgered him with questions about his future. But Tida insisted to them that he would finish college, and Tiger raced back to Stanford. He had an important economics paper due.

Still, it seemed clear Tiger wasn't enjoying himself as much as he used to. Going back and forth between school and golf meant he couldn't devote himself to either. His schedule was so hectic, he didn't even have time for a girlfriend.

Besides, college golf could not have seemed much of a challenge anymore. There simply was no player who could beat him. And college financial regulations for athletes seemed frustrating and narrow. Tiger must have begun to ask himself if he had anything to lose by leaving school. After all, he could earn a lot of money if he turned pro, not just by winning tournaments but also by endorsing products.

In June, he went off to Chattanooga, Tennessee, to play in the NCAA (National Collegiate Athletic Association) golf championship. Nearly 15,000 fans—a tournament record—showed up. In the final round, the gallery was so big, fifteen men had to guard him.

All over the golf course, people had a new feeling about golf. Something was happening to the game, and it was because of Tiger. People who had never followed the sport before were eager to watch it. Even kids were showing up to see him play.

Fans never knew what was going to happen when Tiger swung a club. He could hit a drive 380 yards—that's 1,140 feet, three times longer than a Junior Griffey home run! Even if the ball was in a bunker, Tiger could slash it out and knock it into the cup. No putt was too far away for him to make.

People kept their eyes glued on him. They wanted to touch him, shake his hand, or cheer him on. Some shouted "Kill 'em, Tiger!" or "You go, T!" Fans constantly asked him to autograph everything from hats to scorecards. Ever polite, Tiger often responded, "No problem." He'd high-five kids and throw them balls he wasn't going to use. In the midst of cheers, he'd thank people for rooting him on.

At Chattanooga, Tiger seemed a little nervous. He bogeyed five holes in a row (a "bogey" is one stroke over par). But he was so much better than the competition, he still won by four strokes.

After the championship, his life didn't slow down. Just before the U.S. Open in June, Tiger rushed to complete an accounting term paper and took a final exam in African literature. Then he immediately flew to Detroit, where he started the Open off well. But his concentration failed him—the last five holes were a disaster. No matter what he did, he couldn't putt the ball into the cup.

Tiger seemed furious with himself. After the final round, he lost his temper. Loading his car in the parking lot, he slammed the trunk, slapped his foot on the gas, and roared away. He hated losing tournaments he felt he should have won.

The idea of becoming a pro must have looked more and more attractive at that moment.

When the British Open started in July, Tiger was there, rocketing low, hard drives to avoid the wind. In the second round, he shot a 66—a terrific score on a difficult course. He was learning to slow the speed of his swing and his body, and had more ball control than ever. By the time the tournament was over, Tiger had tied the Open record for the lowest score by an amateur (271). Later he said, "Something really clicked that day, like I had found a whole new style of playing. I finally understood the meaning of playing within myself. Ever since, the game has seemed a lot easier."

The U.S. Amateur was next. Tiger was going for three wins in a row. If he managed that, there was nothing left for him to accomplish in amateur golf. Turning pro was a way to make the game exciting again. It would be a challenge to always go up against the best.

The time for a decision was close at hand.

13

THREE-PEAT

August 1996. The Pumpkin Ridge Golf Club in Cornelius, Oregon. The U.S. Amateur was about to start. But most people weren't talking about the tournament. Rumors were flying that Nike, the sneaker and sportswear giant, had made Tiger an offer he couldn't refuse. Nike was based only fifteen miles from Pumpkin Ridge, and the company's president was in the gallery. Everyone knew Tiger couldn't accept money or endorse any product unless he left Stanford and turned pro.

But as he teed off, Tiger seemed focused on just one thing—winning. He was determined to pull off a genuine golfing feat—to become the first man to "three-peat" the Amateur. With 15,000 fans lining the fairways and crowding the greens, Tiger was playing for history.

And play he did, shooting six beautiful rounds to qualify for the final. Tiger's caddy helped out—this time it was Bryon Bell, Tiger's best friend from high school.

The Sunday of the thirty-six-hole final, Tiger put on a red polo shirt (red is the color he wears when he expects victory). His hat was all black except for an American flag and the words U.S. AMATEUR. In his dark pants and silver belt, he looked very graceful.

But he wasn't golfing that way. After the first nine holes, Tiger was four strokes down. Things just got worse—he was five down after twenty holes. It looked as if Steve Scott, his opponent, would run away with the championship.

Could Tiger have been nervous? After all, he once said, "Every tournament I play in, I have butterflies." And the pressure on him to set an Amateur record was enormous. But as time began to run out, Tiger got down to work. His will to win was so tremendous that by the 27th hole, he was only one stroke behind.

Steve Scott, though, wouldn't let up. On the 28th hole, he made what looked like an impossible shot. Now he was two up on Tiger. That's when he made a mistake. Eager to beat Tiger at last, Steve jumped in the air and pumped his fist. It was a move that apparently made Tiger angry.

A determined look spread over his face. He said, "I was feeling a little heated." On the very next hole, Tiger hit a 350-yard drive, a 180-yard approach shot, and a 45-foot putt. Eagle (two under par)! Tiger was making a point—he'd come back and beat Steve.

Steve didn't panic. He outplayed Tiger over the next four holes. By the time the two rivals had completed the 33rd, Steve was two strokes ahead once more.

Steve studied Tiger. Maybe he thought Tiger looked discouraged. After all, Tiger was keeping his head down as he walked to the 34th hole. But Tiger wasn't discouraged.

Tiger was gathering his strength. He was mentally reaching down inside himself for everything his body had. As if to show Steve what he was made of, he birdied the 34th hole. Now, with just two holes to play, Tiger was one stroke down.

But after Tiger teed off on the 35th, it looked as if all the determination in the world wouldn't be enough. His approach shot was poor, and scooted thirty-five feet wide of the pin. Yet he had to make the hole in just one shot if he was going to tie Steve. Wasn't sinking a thirty-five-foot putt with the stress of a championship at stake an impossible task even for Tiger Woods?

At first, Tiger seemed visibly angry and frustrated. How could he have made such a bad shot? Then he quickly pulled himself together. There was no way he was going to give in to doubt. He swept his putter around and gave the ball a good knock. Steve watched carefully. He probably didn't think Tiger had a chance.

But as the ball traveled toward the cup, Tiger's eyes grew wide. The shot had felt just right. It was going in!

Tie! Tiger shouted for joy and pumped his right fist into the air. Later, he said, "That's a feeling I'll remember for the rest of my life." Steve stood very still, muttering, "Unbelievable."

After the 36th hole, the tournament was still

tied. Now it was playoff time. Who would crack first?

It came down to the 38th hole. That's where Tiger sensed he could win it. Par was three, and Steve couldn't find the cup with his third stroke. Now Tiger would take the trophy if he succeeded where Steve couldn't.

With his six-iron (a club that's one of the medium irons), he hit a drive that dropped just twelve feet short of the pin. He went for the win with his first putt—but he missed. The ball was close, though—only eighteen inches away. One short putt, and he'd set a record.

Tiger stayed calm and focused, and tapped the ball gently. It rolled to the hole—and dropped in. His arms shot into the air. *Victory!*

Oddly enough, Tiger didn't feel excited. In fact, he wasn't feeling much of anything—he was numb. For the last few holes, his concentration had been so intense, he couldn't even remember his shots. But he told reporters, "Given the circumstances, this has to be the best I've ever played."

Only twenty years old, he had just become the greatest amateur golfer ever.

PRO

Three days later, Tiger hopped on a Nike private jet. He landed in Milwaukee, Wisconsin, to make an announcement. With his father beside him, he strode into a tent where a crowd of reporters waited. The first thing he did was smile and say, "I guess, Hello, world."

Tiger had come to Wisconsin to play in the Milwaukee Open. It was a tournament for professionals—and Tiger was turning pro! "Hello, world" was the slogan Nike had invented to launch its Tiger Woods line.

Before he'd even played a shot as a pro, Tiger had an agent and endorsement contracts. He'd signed deals with Nike and a company called

Titleist, which makes golf balls and clubs. Together the contracts were worth over $60 million for five years. Overnight, Tiger had become a multimillionaire.

At his press conference, Tiger explained he hadn't left school just for the money. "It was about happiness," he insisted as reporters scribbled notes and photographers snapped pictures. "I've always dreamed of doing [this], ever since I was a little kid watching Nicklaus on TV." In front of the cameras, he promised Earl and Tida that one day he'd graduate from college.

Tiger also said he turned pro to open up the game. Now he had the same opportunity baseball's Jackie Robinson had—to integrate a sport that discriminated against people of color. Because of his race, Tiger went on, "I don't think I would have been able to play in these tournaments [back in the 1960s]....Now we have an opportunity to get more diversity in such a great game."

As good parents, Tida and Earl had spent years protecting Tiger from prejudice. They'd taught him to be proud of everything he was—African, Asian, and American. More than anything, he believed, "The critical and fundamental point is that ethnic background...should not make a difference."

But being a professional changed things. He was the first black or Asian with a chance to dominate golf. As a superstar, he could turn a white game into a multicultural sport. If he became the champion he wanted to be, he'd end up making history, not just as a sports hero but as a cultural symbol. By bringing blacks and Asians to the links, many for the first time, Tiger would shape golf into a truly American sport at last.

He told reporters he planned to pay special attention to underprivileged kids. Aware he could be a role model for them, Tiger stated he hoped "to help the youth in the inner city and get them playing if they choose to play golf." He knew there were no golf courses in poor urban neighborhoods, so he intended to give clinics (demonstrations and lessons) to get kids started.

Tiger's decision to turn pro was big news. All across the country, reporters and fans were excited. But most golf professionals didn't take Tiger seriously. They felt he was still a kid, with a lot of growing up to do. After all, he was *so* much younger than most of them.

The pros told reporters their game was very different from amateur golf. Since everyone was good, a player couldn't win just by parring holes. Day in and day out, a man had to play at the highest level. With a lot of money at stake, the pressure was severe.

How good, the pros asked, would Tiger be against the best? He'd never been tested, and who knew how he'd deal with the strain? There were those who didn't think he'd even make the PGA tour. After all, an athlete couldn't just go out and play where and when he wanted. He had to qualify for the tour, either by finishing in the top 125 of all golfers (and winning approximately $150,000), by getting special endorsements to play in certain events, or by playing at the PGA Tour Qualifying School (Q-School) in December. This was a tough process called "earning your card."

Earl didn't agree with what the pros were saying. It seemed to him they didn't realize just how good Tiger was. He got them angry when he warned, "You don't want to tangle with Tiger on a golf course. He's what I visualize in the Old West as a black gunslinger. He'll cut your heart out in a heartbeat and think nothing of it."

The pros thought Earl was just a proud father bragging about his son. They weren't ready for what was going to happen next.

15

THE TIGER TOUR

A day after his announcement, Tiger made his professional debut at the Brown Deer Park Golf Course in Milwaukee. It was August 29, 1996. A record crowd of 20,000 stood six rows deep to watch him. On each hole, the gallery stretched all the way from the tee to the green. So many fans surrounded Tiger, Tida couldn't see him. She joked, "I think the only way to watch my Tiger now is on TV."

Some athletes would have been bothered by the hordes of people. Not Tiger. He laughed, "If you lose a ball, there are a lot of people out there to help you find it."

Right away, the packed gallery noticed two

things about him. Among his black shoes, black cap, striped polo shirt, and dark pants, he had sixteen Nike logos spread out over his outfit. And he was so tired, he was yawning between shots.

No one seemed to mind. From start to finish, Tiger thrilled them. His first shot as a pro went 336 yards. In the final round, he smashed a hole in one. Almost as excited as the crowd, Tiger fished the ball out of the cup and tossed it to a fan.

But he wasn't playing well. His fatigue prevented him from concentrating. Shooting a seven-under-par 277, he finished the tournament tied for sixtieth. His first check was for only $2,544.

Were the pros right? Tiger probably didn't think so. His faith in himself was strong, and he wasn't one to waste time worrying. When he finished eleventh in his second event, the Canadian Open, he must have sensed he was on his way.

His third pro tournament was the Quad City Classic in Coal Valley, Illinois. Because Tiger was playing, the largest crowd in club history filed in—over 100,000 fans. They were Asians and blacks, Latinos and whites, young and old, male and female—a different kind of gallery from the ones golf had seen before. Some fans had driven more than 300 miles, lugging along stepladders so they could see over the throng. Excitement was high, as if this were the Super Bowl. Children lining the links imitated Tiger's swing. Even caddies for other golfers came back to watch Tiger when they were finished.

All these people knew something about Tiger the pros hadn't figured out—here was an athlete who wasn't much more than a kid turning a sleepy game for adults into a prime-time event. Tiger was only twenty—but he was a star.

Tiger was in first place for a while, but blew the lead. He ended up finishing fifth, and chalked up his loss to experience. Disappointed but not discouraged, he said, "What I did is part of a learning process."

As if to prove it, he fought hard in his next tournament. Held in Endicott, New York, the B.C. Open was usually a low-key event. But not this year. It was *packed* with fans, reporters, and photographers, all there for a look at Tiger. The event had sold out long before, but people refused to go away. They waited outside the club with signs reading I NEED TICKETS.

Inside, it was a mob scene. The gallery scampered about, climbing buildings and rocks to get a glimpse of Tiger. Other golfers had to plead with them to stand still so they could take their shots. Swarms of people chanted "Tiger, Tiger," flocking around him whenever they could. Once, a twelve-year-old girl cried out "I love you," and Tiger glanced her way. Her girlfriend shouted, "Oh, my God! He looked at you!" Tiger was an idol. He hadn't won a pro tournament yet, but reporters starting calling the PGA schedule "the Tiger Tour."

He did well at the B.C. Open, placing third. That gave him enough earnings to make the PGA tour. In just four events, he'd proved the pros wrong. But that didn't satisfy Tiger. He wanted to be at the top of his game, and he wasn't even close.

In the clubhouse after the tournament, he threw his hat around and cursed. He'd lost because he wasn't sinking his short putts. His swing had slowed, and he wasn't driving the ball straight. So instead of taking a needed rest, he went out and practiced harder.

Now that he was a pro, Tiger seemed to be even more intense about golf. The game seemed to be on his mind every minute of the day. He never wanted to skip practice—even in the pouring rain, he'd be out on the driving range. Unwilling to waste an instant, he'd practice at home, putting the ball against table legs.

But sometimes Tiger was lonely. There was no one his age on the tour. He listened to Montell Jordan and hip-hop, and thought about Stanford and his college friends. "What I miss," he remarked, "is going to a buddy's house or a dorm at eleven at night and just hanging out."

That part of his life was over. Tiger had chosen a new path. He was out to prove he could be the world's best golfer. It wasn't money he was after. "I want to win," he stated. "That's just my nature."

16

THE PHENOM

October 1996. Tiger arrived in Las Vegas, Nevada, on Nike's private jet. He had come to play in the Las Vegas Invitational, his fifth pro tournament. The world's top golfers were here— this was a big-money event. Tiger knew it would be a tough field to beat.

From his penthouse suite at the MGM Grand, he had a great view of the city. There was a TV in every room, and a private elevator only he could use. He was getting the star treatment, and he must have wanted to show the pros he deserved it. This was a tournament he badly wanted to win.

After the first round, though, it didn't look as

if it would happen. Tiger shot just a 70, which left him in eighty-third place. But he came out with his clubs blazing, and by Sunday, was tied for seventh. His confidence was high. He was only four strokes down.

When he walked out on the course for the final round, fans saw he was limping. Tiger had pulled a muscle and was frowning from the pain. But he just bore down—no injury was going to stop him. By the end of the round, Tiger had shot a 64. He was tied with Davis Love III, a top pro, for the lead.

For the first time as a professional, Tiger was in a playoff. He went to the practice tee, grabbed a three-wood (one of the clubs called a wood that are used to hit long shots), and hit a few shots. Butch was there to watch him, along with Fluff Cowan, Tiger's new caddy. As they discussed strategy, Tiger was cool as could be. He neatly peeled a banana and ate it for energy.

The playoff was quick. As fans screamed his name, Tiger triumphed on the 1st hole. Davis shook his hand and said, "You deserved it."

Tiger had done it! Tida was in the crowd, and he called out, "Come here, Mom." Embracing him, she told him, "I'm so proud of you." He raised his trophy high above his head, then signed autographs.

Finally, it was time to go. Tiger got into a stretch limousine. That night, he celebrated his first professional victory with a special dinner. Sipping champagne, he downed two McDonald's cheeseburgers.

There was no stopping Tiger now.

17

ON A ROLL

The Tiger Tour continued. Two weeks later, he was in Orlando, Florida, for the Disney Classic. Everyone was still talking about his Las Vegas win. Tiger, though, was thinking about sweeping *this* event.

It took him a whole round to get down to business. After the first day, he was tied for fifty-eighth place, but on the second, he was a mere two shots off the lead. By the fourth round, he was only one stroke behind.

Just as in Las Vegas, something went wrong the final day. Tiger's throat was sore and his nose stuffed up—it seemed as if he was getting the flu. But all the illness did was make him concentrate harder. In his flaming red shirt, he locked up his second win in his first seven pro events—the greatest professional start in golf history.

By the end of 1996, he'd had the most remarkable rookie season of all time. *Sports Illustrated* named him Sportsman of the Year, the youngest athlete ever to earn the honor. He was also voted the PGA Rookie of the Year. He went back to Las Vegas to celebrate his twenty-first birthday.

Tiger had everyone talking. Golf had always seemed like a game players had to grow into. As an athlete matured, he got better and better. But here was Tiger, not much more than a kid, besting his elders as though it were the easiest thing in the world. One pro said, "Tiger is stunning all of us."

And he'd only just begun.

The 1997 pro season started with the Mercedes Championship at the La Costa Resort and Spa in Carlsbad, California. The winner would take home $296,000 *and* a brand-new Mercedes. With that kind of prize, the world's best golfers showed up.

So did Tiger. The weather was miserable—the rain just wouldn't stop. By January 12, the course was so soaked that only one hole was playable. So tournament officials did the only thing they could—they canceled the eighteen-hole final and made it a sudden-death playoff. Tiger and Tom Lehman, the 1996 Player of the Year, would vie for first.

As usual, the rain didn't keep Tiger from practicing. But it was so wet outside, the driving range was slippery. Fluff wasn't able to keep Tiger's clubs dry. Yet Tiger stayed out there, stroking shot after shot.

The weather didn't keep the fans away either. As the playoff began on the three-par 7th hole, there were hundreds of people standing there under bright umbrellas. They were willing to get drenched for a chance to see Tiger play.

The tee box of the 7th hole was at the top of a rise. The fairway sloped down until it reached the green. On the left was a water hazard, a good-sized pond. The key to winning was to avoid the water.

Tom was the first to start. Right away, he was unlucky. He jerked his swing, and then the wind whisked his ball into the pond. It came down with a splat, sending a flock of birds scooting into the air.

Tom's shoulders slumped. He was in trouble. It was Tiger's turn now, and he was ready to play. Off came his black jacket. His red shirt was the brightest thing on the course. With his usual calm, he took a practice swing. "All I thought about," he reported later, "was where I wanted my ball to go."

A seven-iron (a club that often gives a shot plenty of backspin) in his hands, he drove the ball hard. It landed just six inches from the pin. The crowd roared. They knew this tournament was over.

Tiger tapped his putt in. Victory! Now he had three wins in nine appearances. His prize money added up to over a million dollars. No one had ever won so much so fast on the PGA tour. He was proud of himself—winning, he told reporters, "is what I set out to do." To celebrate, he drank a glass of champagne, and gave the Mercedes to Tida.

The word about Tiger spread throughout America. When he went to a driving range in

Arizona to practice for the Phoenix Open, four bodyguards were needed to get him through the throng. During the actual tournament, fifteen men had to escort him from hole to hole.

He didn't disappoint the Phoenix fans. At the 16th hole of the third round, the gallery of 20,000 was especially loud. Tiger didn't let it bother him. He teed off with a nine-iron. The ball took off, then bounced twice—and plopped right in the cup. Hole in one!

It seemed as if every fan on the fairway went wild. Some reporters said they thought it was the loudest cheer in golf history. Tiger was so delighted, he high-fived a number of fans. As he headed for the 17th hole, one young man jumped onto the green and bowed down before him.

Later, Tiger said, "I don't really remember anything, because I kind of went crazy myself. It was amazing. People were just going crazy. It's ridiculous how loud it was."

The hole in one was Tiger's second as a pro, and the tenth of his career. A hole in one is quite an achievement—some of today's best golfers have never pulled off the feat.

As if stardom in America weren't enough,

Tiger flew off and conquered Asia in February 1997. He was competing in the Asian Honda Classic held at the Thai Country Club in Bangkok, Thailand. Tiger had always called Thailand "my other home" because his mother had been born there.

Before he'd even stroked a shot, the Thais were treating Tiger like a hero. His arrival was such an event that all five Thai TV networks broadcast it live. Over a thousand fans came to the airport to greet him. When Tiger emerged from the plane, they covered him with necklaces of red and yellow flowers.

The tournament began the very next day. It was a sweltering 95 degrees, and Tiger had slept only two hours. Between the heat and his jet lag, he couldn't even finish the first round. Had he come all this way just to get sick?

All of a sudden, Tiger seemed to pull himself together and he began to play well. Perhaps he felt he couldn't disappoint Tida. As it turned out, stroking terrific shots was easier than getting to the golf course! So many fans turned out to see him, he had to take a helicopter to the links. At his hotel, six guards watched over him. No guests were allowed to stay on his floor. Even his phone was protected—no one could call unless they knew the secret password.

There wasn't much competition for Tiger at the tournament. On February 9, he won it by ten strokes. Afterward, the Prime Minister of Thailand made him a citizen of the country.

Being in Thailand with Tida was fun. Tiger visited relatives and gave clinics for kids. But in just a few days, he was back in Orlando, Florida, his new home. The Masters was coming up—his first major tournament as a professional. Weeks of hard work lay ahead of him as he got ready for the event. He planned to play in additional PGA tournaments—it would be good practice.

Tiger was looking forward to the Masters. He knew no one as young as he was had ever won it. Not even Jack Nicklaus.

Were more records about to fall?

18

THE BIG ONE

Spring 1997. Tiger's game was off. The twenty-one-year-old whiz kid so absorbed in his sport was not playing well. Was the PGA tour proving too much for him?

Tiger wasn't focused, and there was a good reason. Sixty-four-year-old Earl was very sick. He was in the hospital and had to have dangerous heart surgery.

Keeping the ball on the fairway wasn't so important to Tiger right now. The tough guy who hated to lose had other things on his mind. He dropped out of one tournament and played poorly in two others.

Earl was lucky—his surgery went well. He

was up and about in a few weeks. So Tiger went happily back to work—getting ready for the Masters. More than any other tournament, this was the one he wanted to win. He'd been dreaming about it ever since he was a kid.

It would be Tiger's third Masters appearance but his first as a professional. It would be the first in which he wasn't also attending school. Butch felt the difference as he helped Tiger train. He said, "Everything we've done this year, all year, has been geared for the Masters." By April, Tiger felt so prepared that he knew he had a good chance to win.

Somehow Tiger sensed he and the Masters were made for each other. He clobbered the ball so far, he made Augusta's long holes seem that much closer. His strength, along with his skill in controlling the speed of his putts, made him one of the tournament favorites.

But there were experts and pros who still doubted Tiger. Could he rein in his power, or would he try to reach the pin with booming drives that shot out of control? Was his putting touch soft enough for the slick greens? After all, Tiger had only played the course twice before.

Experience counted—only those who knew Augusta well had ever won the Masters.

There was another reason experts challenged him, and Tiger knew what it was. He had yet to win a major tournament. Until he took one of the Grand Slam events—the Masters, the U.S. Open, the British Open, or the PGA Championship—some people would believe his reputation was mostly hype.

Tiger tried not to let people's comments bother him. He insisted, "I don't care what anyone else says—as always. I'm just here to win." But there was only way to prove himself once and for all—by wining the green jacket.

On April 10, the sixty-first Masters would start. As tough as Tiger was, Earl and Tida knew he would need their support. So they rented a house in Augusta for the whole family. Tiger invited one of his best friends from Stanford to come along.

Earl still wasn't back to full strength. This time around, he wouldn't be able to follow Tiger from hole to hole. Tida would be there in his place. Earl would sit and watch his son on a TV outside the clubhouse.

On opening day, the weather was sunny—but chilly. With the temperature just 43 degrees, the wind gusted along the links at up to twenty miles per hour. The fans, however, didn't seem to care—the largest gallery ever to see the first round of the Masters piled in. It was so hard to get a ticket, tournament badges were sold illegally for as much as $10,000!

Eighty-six golfers teed off that morning. A first prize of $486,000 was at stake. Tiger didn't give the money a second thought. He was concentrating on his swing—it didn't feel right. Some people wondered if the cool air was bothering him.

On the very first hole, he drove the ball into the pines on the left of the fairway. Then he bogeyed the hole. Things went quickly from bad to worse—by the time he was halfway through the round, he had sent four drives into the pines and had committed four bogeys.

Maybe the experts were right.

At first, Tiger said, "I was pretty hot at the way I was playing." Later he confessed, "I was tight at the beginning....I'm tight every tournament because I care. If you're not nervous, it's because you don't care."

Then on the 10th hole, Tiger stood at the tee and studied the fairway. He decided how to fix his swing—to shorten it. Fluff offered words of encouragement. He told Tiger, "We've got plenty of time to turn this around."

Tiger birdied the 10th. Could he keep it up? The next three holes, called the Amen Corner, are among the hardest in golf to play. Their beautiful flowering trees and bushes stand near deep bunkers and long hazards. One tee box is at the bottom of a hill that is impossible to see over. The 11th, 12th, and 13th holes would be a great test of Tiger's game.

His shortened swing was working. The old smooth stroke was clicking in. Tiger parred the 11th hole, then birdied the 12th and 13th. He was brilliant the rest of the way, ending the round only three strokes off the lead. He admitted, "It was a tough day initially, but I got through it."

It turned out to be the last time he was behind.

19

GOLFING TO GREATNESS

On Friday, a confident Tiger left the clubhouse for the second round. Earl waved to his son and told him, "Just kick some butt today." Tiger did exactly that, shooting a blazing 66—six under par for the course. A huge gallery of fans followed him, cheering his shots. As usual, he was easy to spot. Fluff was carrying his black Titleist bag with the tiger cover tucked over the driver. Fluff himself was wearing white coveralls with WOODS printed in big green letters on his back.

By the end of the afternoon, Tiger had a lead of three strokes. He told reporters, "I feel very relaxed and very patient....I was proud of the way I played. I didn't force anything."

Day three turned out to be humid, and the sky was gray. It didn't matter to Tiger—his game was smoking. Fans and experts alike couldn't believe how well he was playing. In eighteen holes, he didn't bogey once. Shooting a seven-under-par 65, he had seven birdies. He led the tournament by an amazing nine strokes. One golfer said, "He's blowing the field away."

The fans were going crazy over Tiger. On the practice range at sunset, 1,500 watched in awe as he hit wedge after wedge. They knew they were seeing the next Masters champion.

That night, Tiger relaxed with his friend. In between games of Mortal Kombat and Ping-Pong, he downed burgers and fries. He was loose—and ready for tomorrow.

Sunday was cloudy. Gusts of wind flapped the yellow flags on the greens madly. Dressed for victory, Tiger wore a red Nike shirt and dark pants. Butch and Tida were in red, too.

As he came out of the clubhouse surrounded by guards, Tiger knew this could be a historic day. If he held on and won the Masters, he'd be the youngest man, and the first person of color, to do so. Millions of people were cheering him on—millions who had traditionally been shut out of the game. In a sense, they were out there with him. He wasn't alone on the links.

When he approached the teeing ground, Tiger saw clusters of black faces in the mostly white crowd. The clubhouse porch was lined with black employees of the Augusta National. Down the first fairway, a group of black caddies stood and cheered. They all felt Tiger belonged to them—he was their hero.

There was another hero at Augusta that day—someone Tiger deeply admired. Lee Elder, the first black man ever to play at the Masters, had come to see Tiger win. Lee wished Tiger luck, and Tiger commented, "That really reinforced what I had to accomplish. He was the first. It was because of people like him that I was able to turn pro, to get this opportunity."

It was time to tee off. Despite his big lead, Tiger had to stay focused. Looking as calm as if this were a practice round, he parred the 1st hole, then birdied the 2nd. But he couldn't help but feel the pressure. He bogeyed the 5th hole, and then the 7th.

Suddenly, Tiger's game clicked back in.

Perhaps he remembered what Earl had told him about today—this would be the toughest round of his life, but all he had to do was play like himself. He birdied the 8th, the 11th, the 13th, and the 14th holes. Now he could set a record for the lowest Masters score ever. All he had to do was maintain par the rest of the way.

The afternoon was drawing to a close. Tiger felt chilly. With his red sweatshirt on, he played the 15th, 16th, and 17th holes. Each one was par.

He stayed intense. After a shot, he'd talk out loud, scolding himself or urging himself on. Often he'd turn and discuss strategy with Fluff. Then he'd towel off his club and stroke the ball where he wanted.

Everywhere fans stood and clapped and cheered for Tiger. The ovations were so long, it was as though no one wanted to stop. Leaning forward to see him, people sometimes got close enough to touch him. Grinning widely, Tiger slapped their palms and tipped his hat. But he never stopped working toward the record.

At last, Tiger was playing the 18th hole. He took a deep breath and jabbed the tee into the ground. This was it, for the Masters and the history books.

As he teed off, a camera clicked twice, loudly. Caught off-guard by the noise, Tiger jerked his swing. The ball hooked left off the fairway as he glared over his shoulder. He spat out one word, "Please."

Fluff calmed him down. He told Tiger, "Let's go find [the ball] and enjoy this walk anyway."

So Tiger did.

He wandered into the gallery in search of his ball. Fans swarmed around him, whistling and roaring. Security guards tried to move them, but everyone wanted to congratulate Tiger. Finally, he spotted the ball.

But he still couldn't take the shot. So many people surrounded him, he couldn't find Fluff! As though he were on a trampoline, Tiger jumped up and down crying his caddy's name. The crowd shouted "Fluff! Fluff!" to help out. Fluff reappeared.

This next shot was crucial. To get the record, Tiger had to make par. But if he didn't get the ball up on the green, he wouldn't have a chance.

Tiger decided to use his wedge. The crowd got very quiet. He stroked the ball brilliantly. It landed just twelve feet from the cup!

The gallery cheered once more. Tiger was beaming. But his mind stayed on the game—there was so much at stake. As he moved to the ball, he remembered the black golfers who had come before him, the three who had played here once, and the countless great ones who had been denied. He revealed later, "I said a little prayer of thanks to those guys."

Only two more strokes for par. Fluff removed the yellow flag from the pin. Tiger's first putt passed by the hole. Miss! But his next, a five-footer, dipped in. Par! He'd taken the Masters and set a record!

Tiger's achievement left both experts and pros reeling. He hadn't just won the Masters—he had overwhelmed his competition. With his fourth-round score of 69, his eighteen-under-par 270 was the lowest Masters score ever. His nearest opponent was twelve strokes behind—no one had *ever* had a larger margin of victory. The youngest man ever to triumph here, he was also the first person of color to wear the green jacket.

In fact, he was the only person of color to ever win a major golf championship. He'd averaged 323 yards on his drives—25 yards more than the runner-up. And he'd accomplished it all as a PGA tour rookie!

Tiger punched the air with his right fist. He threw his arms around Fluff. Then he walked off the green and up to his parents. Tears pouring down his face, he hugged Earl tightly. Tida stroked his arm and wept too.

The dream had come true.

THE GREEN JACKET

Tiger had shown an entire nation his physical power, his mental toughness, and his athletic talent. Golfing records weren't the only ones he broke—more people watched the Masters on TV than ever before. Even the President called to congratulate Tiger.

He couldn't stop smiling when he was presented with the green jacket. Earl commented, "Green and black go well together, don't they?" Another racial barrier had fallen at last.

Tiger was quick to pay tribute to the black golfers who came before him. "It means so much. I'm the first, but I wasn't the pioneer. Charlie Sifford, Lee Elder, Teddy Rhodes—those guys paved the way for me to be here. I thank them. If it wasn't for them, I might not have had the chance to play here."

In all the excitement, Tiger looked for one man in particular. At last he spotted him and embraced him. It was Lee Elder. Tiger said to him, "Thanks for making this possible."

In the evening, Tiger was the guest of honor at a victory dinner at the clubhouse. Every Masters winner becomes an automatic member of the Augusta National Golf Club. He was happy and proud, but he couldn't forget the past. Here he was, a black and Asian face in an almost completely white crowd. He didn't have to swing a golf club to stick out here.

One day, that will be different. Tiger Woods and his victories have changed golf forever.

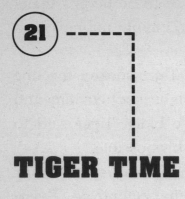

TIGER TIME

What's next for Tiger? No one can be sure. But there's already talk of his winning the Grand Slam. No golfer in modern history has ever done that. But after his Masters victory, experts wonder if Tiger could. Tiger himself says, "It can be done."

After all, it would fit in perfectly with his goal to become the greatest golfer ever. Jack Nicklaus has eighteen major golf championships, including six Masters. But Nicklaus himself thinks Tiger can win more.

Some pros agree. One calls him the most important player of the last fifty years. The PGA commissioner goes even further. He says Tiger "might be the most important player *ever.*"

What's clear is that a new era has dawned in golf. It's Tiger Time. If anyone can make the game popular all across the country, it's Tiger.

But what a burden he has, living up to these expectations. He's been hyped more than any other young athlete. It's true he's had to grow up fast, but still, he's so young—will he burn out or get injured? After all, he was a star at twenty in a sport where most athletes don't reach their prime until their thirties. Will he get bored with the game? People who know Tiger say never. He himself says golf is "like a drug. If I don't have it, I go crazy…. I've got to keep playing."

Still, being Tiger the superstar isn't easy. The press has its eye on his every move. When he makes a mistake, he has to read all about it. There's nowhere he can go without being recognized. He's even getting a private plane so he can travel in peace.

As golf's first black and Asian superstar, Tiger is well aware that he's a role model. He makes a point of conducting clinics at public golf courses in big cities like Boston, Chicago, and

Los Angeles. Twenty-five hundred children showed up at his clinic in Phoenix!

While he particularly likes to encourage black kids to learn golf, he wants to reach out to everyone. "It doesn't matter," he insists, "whether they're white, black, brown, or green. All that matters is I touch kids the way I can through clinics and they benefit from them."

Money hasn't spoiled him. He still wears his Mickey Mouse watch and eats at McDonald's. One of the ways he enjoys his wealth is helping people. In January 1997, Tiger started the Tiger Woods Foundation. The foundation will aid poor children, in America and abroad, through golf. Tiger says, "Golf is basically a vehicle for me to help people....That's the main thing—that I can touch people, that I can inspire their lives in a positive way...being able to help people and give back. That's what it's all about."

While he says he'll be a happy man if he can "hit the perfect shot," Tiger wants more. To be the world's best golfer. To end racial and ethnic discrimination in his sport. To make sure kids "think golf is cool."

And if anyone can do it, Tiger Woods can.